by JANE THAYER

PICTURES BY SEYMOUR FLEISHMAN

WILLIAM MORROW AND COMPANY
NEW YORK • 1964

With love, to Mary Ann.

What Mary Ann liked best in school
was studying dinosaurs.
She knew the name of every kind.
She could spell allosaur and megalosaur.
She had dinosaur models.
She had read dinosaur books.
"If I could just find
one dinosaur!" she said.

Mary Ann lived near a mountain.
Whenever she climbed the mountain,
she looked for dinosaurs.
She happened to be passing
a cave on the mountain one day
when she saw something sticking out.
It looked like a dinosaur's tail.

She took hold of the tail
and gave it two yanks.
Ding, ding.

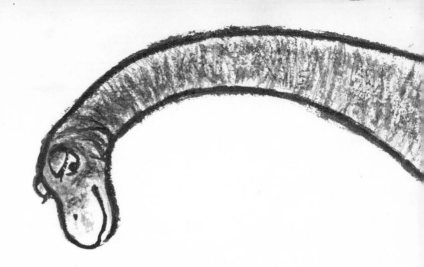

A huge dinosaur came out,
blinking in the sunshine!
He had been sleeping
for sixty million years.
And he was the last dinosaur
left in the world.
"I have found a dinosaur!" said Mary Ann.

She wanted to take him home at once.
The dinosaur seemed pleased
to be going some place,
so they started down the mountain,
the dinosaur marching along.

Suddenly an airplane zoomed overhead.

The dinosaur jerked up his head in alarm.

Mary Ann told him it was only an airplane.

He seemed nervous, but he marched along.

They came to a highway.

They were about to cross the road

when a trailer truck roared by.

The dinosaur jerked up his head

and rolled his eyes.

He seemed very frightened.

Mary Ann told him it was only a truck,

but he still seemed frightened.

Finally he marched along.

They came to a railroad crossing.
Mary Ann was just about
to lead the dinosaur across the tracks
when the warning bell rang—
clang, clang, clang, clang.
The twelve-thirty train
came thundering through
like a roaring rocket.
The dinosaur jerked up his head,
rolled his eyes,
and leaped back in terror.

"That's only a train!" cried Mary Ann.
But he was so terrified,
he shook all over.
It was quite a while
before she could get him
to calm down
and march along.

They arrived at Mary Ann's house.
When Mary Ann's mother saw the dinosaur,
she said, "Mary Ann, you know better
than to bring that dinosaur home!"
"Can't I keep him for a pet?"
said Mary Ann.
"Certainly not," said her mother.
"What would we do with him
when we went on our vacation?"

"Then I'll take him to school,"
said Mary Ann.
She knew the children
would love to have
a dinosaur for a pet,
and Miss Tutt, the teacher,
was fond of animals too.
Next day she took him to school.

WATCH
OUT FOR
CHILDREN

She went in to tell the class
she had found a dinosaur.
"Is he a brachiosaur,
or a stegosaur,
or a diplodocus?
Where is he?" everyone cried.
"He's a brontosaur.
He's outside," said Mary Ann.
At lunchtime the children rushed out.
"He isn't afraid of us!" they cried.
"May we feed him?"
"Why, certainly," said Miss Tutt.
"You may never meet a dinosaur again."
"What's his name?" cried the children.
Mary Ann looked at
the dinosaur thoughtfully.
"His name is Dandy,"
she decided.

Dandy the dinosaur ate a ham sandwich,
four peanut-butter sandwiches,
a tomato-and-mayonnaise sandwich,
six hard-boiled eggs,
two pickles, a doughnut, seven cookies,
and three chocolate bars.
"May we keep him for a pet Miss Tutt?"
Mary Ann asked.
"Why, certainly," said Miss Tutt.

They put Dandy
in a quiet corner of the schoolyard.
The children fed him.
He seemed happy.
Mary Ann could not believe
she had a pet dinosaur.
Then an unfortunate thing happened.
Someone put the news about Dandy
in the paper.
People began to come for miles to see him.
They came in cars.

They came in trucks.

They came on motorcycles.

They came in sight-seeing planes,
swooping down to take a picture
of Dandy the dinosaur.

Mary Ann and her class
were proud of their pet.
They wanted people to come and see him.
The only trouble was
that the school was very noisy now,
with engines roaring, horns blowing,
and brakes squealing!
Then Mary Ann noticed that Dandy
no longer seemed happy.
She noticed
that he hid his head and trembled
when visitors came.

More and more visitors came.
Finally Dandy
kept his head hidden and shook like a leaf
all the time.
Mary Ann was worried.
What can be wrong
with our poor trembling Dandy?
she thought.
Perhaps I should call up
some famous scientist,
and ask him to come and see what is wrong
with our Dandy, she thought.

She phoned a famous scientist,
named Dr. St. George,
who said he would take the next plane.
Dr. St. George arrived.
He felt Dandy's head.
He counted his pulse.
He looked at his teeth
to see if he had a toothache.
"Perhaps he has
a touch of something," he said.

Just then a man came popping along
on a motorcycle,
to see Dandy the dinosaur.
Dandy jerked up his head,
jumped, and started to run away.
"Perhaps he's afraid of people,"
Dr. St. George said,
as he brought him back.
"He isn't afraid of people at all,"
said Mary Ann.

"I'll watch him for a few days,"
said the famous Dr. St. George.
"Where can we put him
so he won't run away?"
The only place they could think of
was in the gymnasium.
It was quite a job to get him in there,
but Mary Ann and Dr. St. George pushed.

The other children pulled.

When he got inside the gymnasium,

Dandy the dinosaur held up his head.

He looked around.

He stopped trembling.

"He feels better!" cried Mary Ann.

"I think I know

what was wrong!"

At that moment, in the next room,
the school band began to practice.
The band crashed into its loudest piece.

Dandy the dinosaur jumped,
jerked up his head, rolled his eyes,
and almost went through the wall
of the gymnasium.
This time Mary Ann and Dr. St. George
could hardly hold him.

"Stop the band!" shouted Dr. St. George,
holding the dinosaur's tail.
Mary Ann rushed out
and asked the band to stop playing.
The music stopped.
Dandy calmed down at once.
Dr. St. George looked at Mary Ann,
and he nodded wisely.
She nodded back.
"Of course!" said Dr. St. George.
"It's the *noise!*
He has never heard a brass band before."
"Or noisy planes or trucks or trains,"
Mary Ann agreed.

"Sixty million years ago,"
Dr. St. George said,
"all he ever heard
were the wind and the water,
a rock rolling downhill,
and dinosaurs talking."
"I know," said Mary Ann.

"What shall we do now?"
said the famous Dr. St. George.
"*I* know!" said Mary Ann.
She explained to the other children
that Dandy
was afraid of only one thing—
a loud noise.

So the children made a sign,
which they put up in front of the school.
It said:

Then the school became quiet again.
When the people saw the sign,
they parked their cars in a parking lot
and tiptoed up to the dinosaur.
Dandy was delighted to see them,
and crunched Crackerjack.
Mary Ann was a happy girl,
because now she had
dinosaur models and dinosaur books to study,
and Dandy Dinosaur too.

And when Mary Ann grew up,
what do you think she did?
Why, she became
a famous scientist, of course,
like the famous Dr. St. George,
because she knew more about dinosaurs
than anyone else in the world!

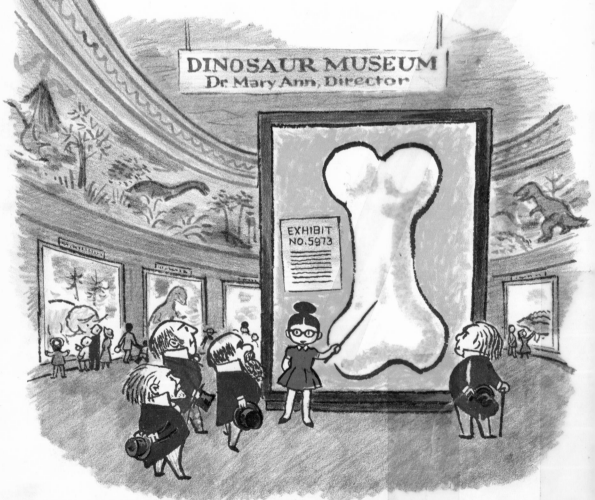